ckets

MY SISTER'S NAME IS
ROVER

Rover
the Champion

Chris Powling and
Scoular Anderson

A & C Black

Rockets

ROVER - Chris Powling and Scoular Anderson

Rover's Birthday
Rover the Champion
Rover Goes to School
Rover Shows Off

First paperback edition 2000
First published 1999 in hardback by
A & C Black (Publishers) Ltd
35 Bedford Row, London WC1R 4JH

Text copyright © 1999 Chris Powling
Illustrations copyright © 1999 Scoular Anderson

The right of Chris Powling and Scoular Anderson
to be identified as author and illustrator of this
work has been asserted by them in accordance with
the Copyright, Designs and Patents Act 1988.

ISBN 0-7136-5200-4

A CIP catalogue record for this book is available
from the British Library.

Printed and bound by G. Z. Printek, Bilbao, Spain.

My sister's name is Rover.
Well... it is when she's wearing the
puppy costume Granpa made for her.

In our house, it's nothing special to see
a dog reading a book.

Or playing
a recorder.

Or having a ride on our garden swing.

In fact, when my sister wasn't wearing her puppy costume she got into a terrific temper.

Take this morning for example.

She wasn't, though.

As he hunched over his old sewing machine, she hopped from foot to foot, huffing and puffing.

At last, Granpa had finished.
'There,' he said. 'One puppy costume
as good as new. Every rip and split
has been mended.'

I suppose that was a thank you.

As soon as she was
back to being Rover,
my sister rushed
outside.

Isn't it good to see
your little sister back
to her old self, Barney?

WOOF!
WOOF!
WOOF!

Suddenly, she spotted Old One Ear.
Old One Ear belonged to grumpy
Mrs Robinson next door. He took one
look at Rover and ran straight up a tree.

Within seconds, Mrs Robinson came charging up the garden path. 'See that, you horrible beast?' she called over the fence.

Rover looked at the cat for a moment.

Then she looked at Mrs Robinson.

Finally, she looked at Granpa's step-ladder lying in the grass.

A moment later she
started climbing.

Mrs Robinson's
mouth fell open.

So was Old One Ear.

Soon, both of them had scuttled indoors for a long, soothing lie down.

I grinned at my sister.

Rover came down the ladder very slowly.
She seemed to be thinking hard.

Later, I saw her crouched by our front gate. She was watching a big, bony Great Dane stroll by. My sister began to copy every move it made.

She did the same with a
French Poodle...

...a small,
snuffly Pekinese...

...a sausage dog...

...and a husky, the sort of dog which pulls a sledge across the frozen North.

As the week went by, I noticed her doing other doggy things too. I decided I'd better have a word with Granpa.

23

Granpa gave me one of his winks.
Did he know something I didn't?

Then I remembered the Village Summer Fete. Wasn't it on this very weekend? Quickly, I fetched the programme from our kitchen noticeboard.

GRAND VILLAGE FETE

ON
BANK
HOLIDAY
MONDAY
· AMUSEMENTS ·
· PONY RIDES ·
· FANCY DRESS CONTEST ·
· EVERY KIND OF STALL
YOU CAN IMAGINE.
· TOMBOLA · RAFFLES · ROUNDABOUTS ·
ETC.

ALSO DOG OF THE YEAR SHOW
AT
4.00 pm
SHARP

Now I understood.

'She's going to gatecrash THE DOG OF
THE YEAR SHOW!' I whispered to myself.
'She really thinks she can win it... even
when she's up against *real* dogs!'

Of course, there was no point in arguing
about it. I could imagine the replies
I'd get.

Granpa would say:

Dog of the year? Well, why not? It's a pretty good puppy costume after all.

Dad would remark:

Remember, she does have acting in the blood. Perhaps she'll fool everybody.

And Mum would finish off:

And you must help her as much as you can, Barney. That's what a Big Brother is for.

Not this Big Brother, thank you.

People came from miles around to our Summer Fete. And they all stayed to watch THE DOG OF THE YEAR SHOW. Why should I let my little sister show me up?

So I came up with a plan.

On the day of the Fete, I was extra-friendly to my sister. After playing with her all morning, I exclaimed,

Hey, I've emptied my piggybank and I've asked Mum and Dad for some early birthday money.

WOOF!

I had to push her away from me in the end.

Right from the start, my plan worked brilliantly. I kept Rover so busy on Fete afternoon, she hardly had time to bark. Mind you, plenty of kids barked for her.

WOOF! WOOF! they called as she whizzed down the helter-skelter.

WOOF! WOOF! they barked as she tried out the pony ride.

WOOF! WOOF! they chanted as she had a go on the coconut shy.

Wherever Rover went, she was followed by WOOF! WOOF! WOOF! from kids who wished they had a puppy costume, too.

Why, I almost wished Granpa had made one for... no, not quite.

I wasn't *that* impressed by the attention.

Besides, who could be better than my sister at this doggy stuff? Only a real dog could beat her now...

Then again, maybe it couldn't. If she missed THE DOG OF THE YEAR SHOW, how would we ever know? I was beginning to have second thoughts.

Shall we give it a try, Rover?

When the clock on the village green struck four, I grabbed her collar.

To my surprise, I almost had to drag her to the Show Ring.

THE DOG OF THE YEAR SHOW
COMPETITORS →

When we got there we just tagged on
behind the other dogs. Their owners
didn't seem to mind a bit.
'Hello, Barney,' they said.
'Hello... er...'

After this, we simply did what they did.

The first judge looked at grooming. This was easy-peasy after Granpa's repairs to the puppy costume.

The second judge looked at obedience.
Rover had no trouble here, either. It was
as if she understood every word I said.

The third judge looked at special tricks.
For Rover, this meant walking on her
back legs.

She was so good, you'd have thought she'd done it all her life.

While this was going on Rover's Fan Club was singing its heart out. From all round the ring came:

No other dog had a chance, really.

I couldn't believe how nice everyone was
when we went up to collect First Prize.
It was presented by a famous actor friend
of Mum and Dad's.

I've never been so proud in my life.
Mum, Dad and Granpa were
pretty pleased, too.

But my sister was tired out. She couldn't
stop yawning.

'Thank you, Barney,' she said sleepily.
'What made you think of putting
me in THE DOG OF
THE YEAR SHOW?'

Suddenly, I felt a bit tired myself.

The End